C000124955

This Expi Book Belongs to:

• •

• •

Nishita Hitesh Bhayani, Author
Expi Elephant Travels to Dubai
© 2022, Nishita Hitesh Bhayani.

Illustrations and Book Design by Leilani Angela Coughlan
3rd Edition

ISBN: 9798371327024

I would like to dedicate this book to
my family; H, A and K - my biggest fans.

- N.B.

For my family and friends
all around the world.

-L.C.

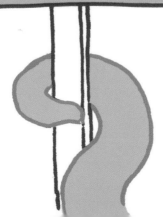

Expi Elephant is her catchy name,
And to win the big prize is her sole aim.
At school there is a quiz to be won,
And a super prize for two which is so much fun!
"I want to win this prize for my Mum you see,
So we can travel the world, Mum and me!"

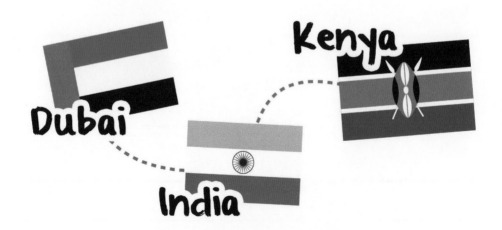

Question Time!

1. Have you entered any competitions at school?

She desperately wants to win
and go the whole yard!

Expi eats chocolate bars with
all of the stress,

With books spread out,
learning for that
geography test!

2. What birthday present would you buy your Mum?

3. What do you spend your pocket money on?

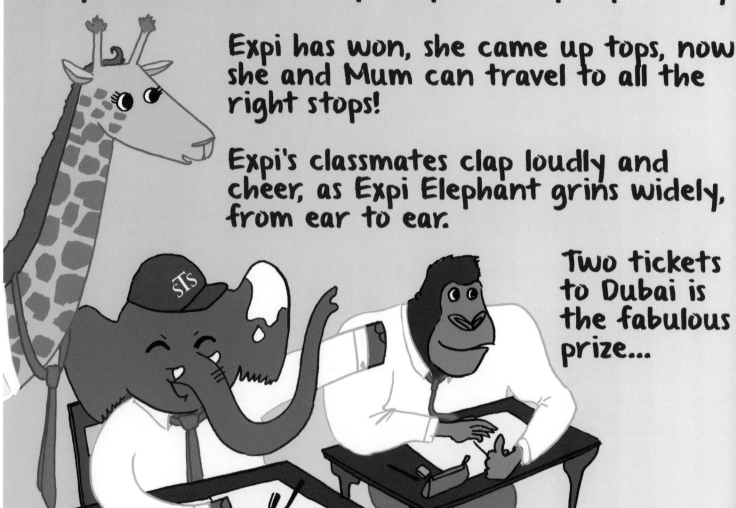

Mr. Hippo - Bottom announces in class the next day, "The winner is Expi Elephant, Hip Hip hooray!

Expi has won, she came up tops, now she and Mum can travel to all the right stops!

Expi's classmates clap loudly and cheer, as Expi Elephant grins widely, from ear to ear.

Two tickets to Dubai is the fabulous prize...

Expi's friends: Jellybean Giraffe, Earz Elephant and GoGo Gorilla

DATE NOV 25th

Question Time!

1. What is Expi's Teacher called?

2. Which subject have they been tested on?

3. What is the name of Expi's school?

Expi rushes home extremely excited you see,
And gifts Mum this prize with glee.

Question Time!

1. What is Expi holding in her trunk?

2. What country would you like to visit if you won a prize like that?

3. How are Expi and Mum feeling?

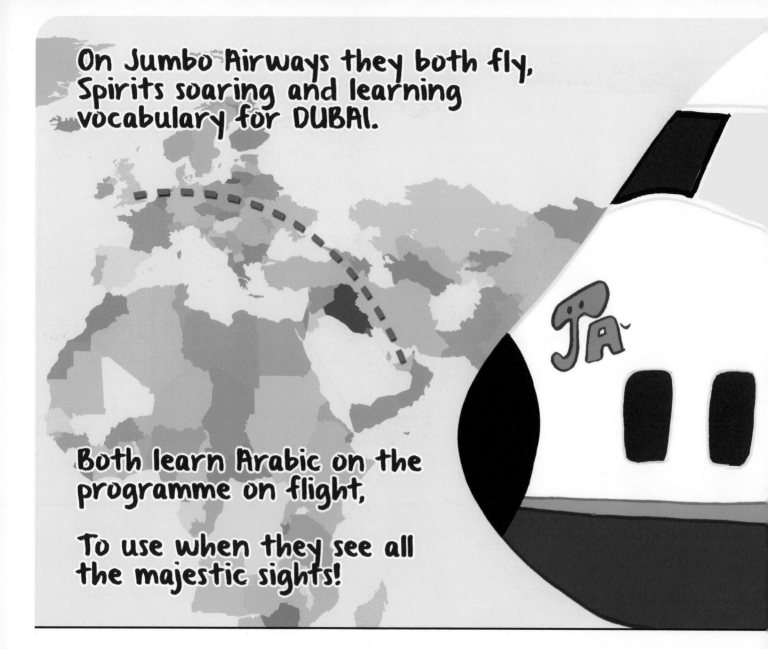

On Jumbo Airways they both fly,
Spirits soaring and learning
vocabulary for DUBAI.

Both learn Arabic on the
programme on flight,

To use when they see all
the majestic sights!

Question Time!

1. What do Expi and Mum do on the flight?

Once in a lifetime is this exceptional trip, let's travel with them and see what's on their list.

2. What languages do they speak in Dubai?

3. How are Expi and Mum feeling?

Question Time!

1. What dishes did Expi and Mum order for their Arabic mezze?

This is followed by a delicious picnic lunch, falafel sandwiches and Baklavas they munch.

"These are yum," says Expi, as one by one

Baklavas are balanced and taken into her tum!

2. What foods do you like to eat at a picnic?

3. What is the famous building that they see?

Question Time!

1. Which beaches have you visited?

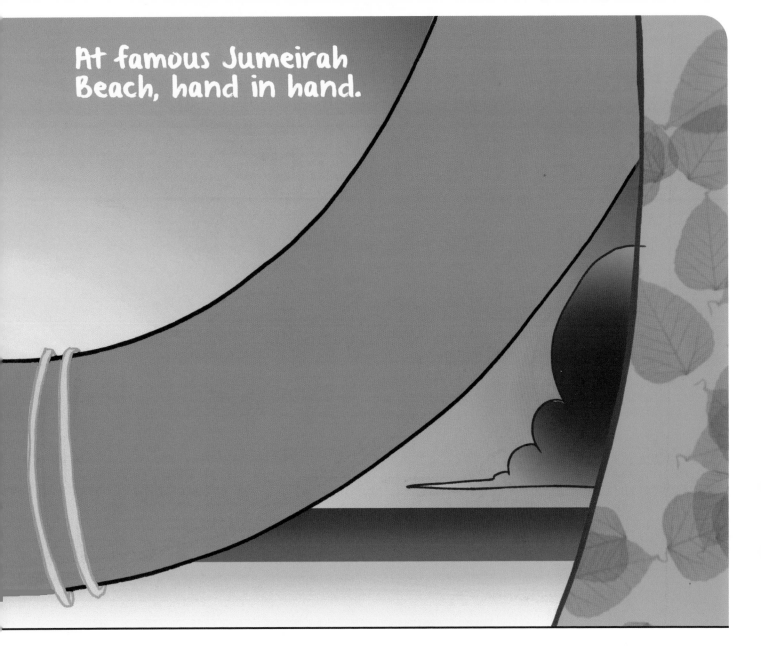

At famous Jumeirah Beach, hand in hand.

2. What do you like to do at the beach?

3. What famous beach are Expi and Mum walking on?

They head downtown as evening falls,

By the Burj Khalifa, they are enthralled.

The tallest building in the world they go to see

Question Time!

1. Which famous building do they go to see?

And experience the musical fountains with glee!

Entranced and spellbound as the fountains dance high.

Expi and Mum give a contented sigh.

2. What is the capital of the United Arab Emirates?

3. Do you know any other tall buildings in Dubai?

The thrilling desert Safari is on for the next day,

In a huge jeep with big wheels, they are on their way.

Question Time!

1. Have you been on a desert safari?

Expi yells, "My stomach is doing flippity - flops!"

As they head up over the sand dunes and then drop.

"My stomach's like a wobbly jelly," shrieks Mum,

"What a four wheel ride, it's jolly good fun!"

2. Can you name a bird that lives in the desert?

3. What would you carry with you into the desert?

Towards evening, they indulge at the busy campsite,

Where they stop for a savouring barbeque bite.

Question Time!

1. Have you tried Henna painting before?

The camp fire is blazing while they watch the dancing show,

Tourists enjoy henna painting while the camp fire glows.

2. What are Expi and Mum eating?

3. How are Expi and Mum feeling?

Question Time!

1. What is the national bird of Dubai?

2. What is the national animal of the UAE?

The Mall of the Emirates is next on their list,

In the Mall a ski and snow park amongst their midst!

"Yippee!" Expi yells, as she sledges down the slope fast,

Question Time!

1. Which famous mall is 'Ski Dubai' in?

Mum watches closely while Expi has a blast!

It's very safe Mum observes as hot chocolate she sips, Expi and Mum are really enjoying this amazing trip!

2. Who has been to 'Ski Dubai'?

3. What do you like to do when it snows?

Question Time!

1. What date is National Day in Dubai?

Celebrations are held all across the land

People come together to make a stand.

Balloons and Flags are waved up high,

As the fast jets whoosh through the night sky.

2. Expi collects flags, do you collect anything?

The atmosphere is friendly and very light,
As fireworks explode marking the special night.

Question Time!

1. What colours make up the UAE flag?

The national colours of black, white, red and green, are all around in Royal Unity to be seen!

"The local people are so nice" and Expi makes friends, with two little Arabic boys and stays till the end.

2. Who does Expi make friends with?

3. What special days do you celebrate with fireworks?

Question Time!

1. What does Expi get Mum for her birthday?

Wanting to take dates and presents back home,

The very last day is spent to have a roam.

The Souk is perfect for trinkets and dates, also for shawls, sweets and spices - A rate!

"I've also got YOU a gold birthday chain, Mum!"

"Oh, Expi! How kind!" says Mum in return.

For her precious little girl, Mum sheds happy tears,

For this unique trip she will remember for years and years!

2. What gifts would you buy from Dubai?

3. What does the word 'souk' mean?

It's time to go back, that time again for school,

Question Time!

1. Which country are they going back to?

They will miss the basking sun and cool pool.

Wonderful sights, hard to compare.

Spending time to relax and time that is rare.

2. What famous buildings have they seen in Dubai?

3. How are they feeling now it's time to go back?

As they sit on the sofa at home and look at their colourful snaps, Dubai in the U.A.E. is marked forever on their map!

DATE **DEC 05**th

Question Time!

1. Which is your favourite place to visit when in Dubai?

Where will they travel to next, do you want to know?

"Take out the globe and point,

Let's all have a Go!"

The End.

2. How many places do Expi and Mum visit whilst in Dubai?

3. Where do you think they travel to next?

The 'Expi Elephant Song'!

Hey everybody, everybody look out
Expi's coming, let's all give a shout
Hey everybody, everybody look out
Expi's coming, let's all give a shout

Chocolate in one and a globe in the other
She wants to give a birthday gift to her mother

Hey everybody, everybody look out
Expi's coming, let's all give a shout

When she checks her money box little comes out
So she studies like never, all give her a shout

Hey everybody, everybody look out
Expi's studying, let's all give a shout
Hey everybody, everybody look out
Expi's studying, let's all give a shout

She wins the big quiz at St. Trunks School
Now Expi and Mum can travel so cool!

Hey everybody, everybody look out
Expi's travelling, let's all give a shout
Hey everybody, everybody look out
Expi's travelling, let's all give a shout

Come with us to experience all of the fun
First to Dubai in the U-A-E sun

Hey everybody, everybody look out
Expi's here, let's all give a shout
Hey everybody, everybody look out
Expi's HERE, let's all give a shout

Watch the 'Expi Elephant Song' on YouTube!

Glossary

Glee - great delight, especially from one's own good fortune

Shukran - Arabic for 'Thank You'

Afwan - Arabic for 'You are welcome'

Baklava - A dessert made of filo pastry, chopped nuts, and syrup or honey

Arabic Mezze - A selection of small plates of Arabic food, dips and salads

Burj Al Arab - The world's only 7-star hotel it is shaped like the sail of a boat

Jumeirah Beach - The beach that runs along the length of the city of Dubai

Burj Khalifa - The tallest building in the world

Hoopoe Bird - A colourful bird with a distinctive 'crown' of feathers

Falcon - A bird of prey that is also the national bird of the UAE

Arabian Oryx - A medium-sized white antelope with very long, straight horns

Henna - Temporary body art resulting from the staining of the skin

Emirati - The name of the peoples who live in Dubai and the UAE

Souk - A market where people buy and sell goods

Mall of the Emirates - One of the most famous malls in Dubai

Ski Dubai - An entire ski slope and adventure park inside Mall of the Emirates

Emirates Palace - The most luxurious hotel in Abu Dhabi

HRH Sheikh Zayed
Founding Father of
the United Arab Emirates

Burj Khalifa
the tallest building in the world

Falcon - the national bird

Dirham
the official currency of the
United Arab Emiarates

Dot-to-Dot

Expi Dubai Wordsearch

N	I	A	R	A	B	I	C	E	O	G	B
A	C	H	J	D	U	T	B	Z	R	A	U
J	K	S	H	U	K	R	A	N	S	F	R
I	F	B	A	P	Q	C	B	B	D	B	J
H	A	L	H	C	G	D	A	O	U	V	A
Q	L	J	A	D	O	S	K	M	N	C	L
G	C	H	R	G	F	E	L	A	E	W	A
R	O	J	I	K	S	L	A	M	S	L	R
X	N	J	E	E	P	X	V	L	E	D	A
W	K	T	M	V	U	Z	A	N	M	Y	B
M	P	Y	U	M	A	F	W	A	N	F	O
B	U	R	J	K	H	A	L	I	F	A	N

1. Falcon
2. Camel
3. Burj Khalifa
4. Jumeirah
5. Jeep
6. Flags
7. Burj Al Arab
8. Arabic
9. Dunes
10. Baklava
11. Afwan

Help Expi and Mum get to the Burj Khalifa!

Can you spot the 8 differences?

Colour-in the scene...

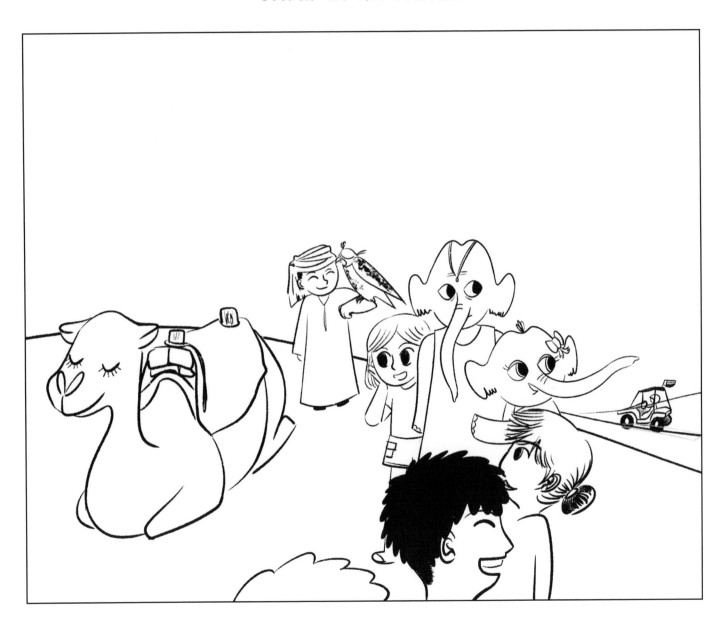

Design your own Firework!

Here are some examples to inspire you!

Fireworks can burst into a whole variety of amazing and wonderful shapes and colours!
What designs have you seen in the Dubai night sky?

Other titles in the Expi Elephant series:

 Expi Elephant Travels to India

 Expi Elephant Travels to Kenya

Independent Author Publishing

Independent Author Publishing
www.independentauthorpublishing.com

Printed in Great Britain
by Amazon

31734642R00027